Ditties for the Nursery

DITTIES
FOR THE NURSERY

"So wonderfully contrived that they may
be either sung or said, by Nurse or Baby."

Edited by
IONA OPIE

Illustrated by
MONICA WALKER

London
OXFORD UNIVERSITY PRESS

Oxford University Press, Amen House, London E.C.4

GLASGOW NEW YORK TORONTO MELBOURNE WELLINGTON
BOMBAY CALCUTTA MADRAS KARACHI KUALA LUMPUR
CAPE TOWN IBADAN NAIROBI ACCRA

First Edition 1954
Reprinted 1959

Printed in Great Britain by
Jesse Broad & Co. Ltd., Old Trafford, Manchester.

Introduction

These are some of the rhymes which delighted children
the reign of George III. They were published about
305 under the title *Original Ditties for the Nursery, So
Wonderfully Contrived that they may be either Sung or Said, by
Nurse or Baby*. The ditties were very popular, and second
nd third editions soon followed. Their publisher, John
arris, was the leading children's bookseller of his day,
successor to the Newberys, and to the " Original Juvenile
Library " at the corner of St. Paul's Churchyard in the
City of London.

Whoever was the author of these ditties he, or she, has a
laim to fame. Among the rhymes which appear in
Ditties for the Nursery are "Tweedledum and Tweedledee",
which Lewis Carroll introduced into *Alice Through the
Looking-Glass*, and " A farmer went trotting upon his
grey mare ", which became renowned when Randolph
Caldecott illustrated it in 1884. As well, " Little Jenny
Flinders ", " Cobbler, cobbler, mend my shoe ", and
In a cottage near Fife", which are still repeated in
present-day nurseries, appeared in print for the first time.
There are other rhymes equally good, including " 'Squire
Frog's Visit ", an excellent version of a song which was
d when the first Queen Elizabeth was a child. If the
compilers of 19th century nursery rhyme collections had
known of the existence of this book there is no doubt that
many more of the ditties would now be universally known.

IONA OPIE

5

This is Tweedledee's rattle before
Tweedledum spoilt it (page 53).
It was a silver rattle, with bells
and a pink coral.

Contents

My Orange

Oh my orange ! my orange !
Why did I leave you behind ?
  For little Sam Spruce
  Has sucked out your juice,
Leaving nothing for me but the rind.

Knee Song

A nimble, an amble ! a nimble, an amble !
    My lady is coming this way ;
She likes better to ride on her pony, than ramble
    Upon her ten toes all the day.

A trot—a trot—a trot—a trot,
　　My lord sits his horse by her side ;
Do you see what a fine hat and feather he's got,
　　To ride with his beautiful bride ?

A canter—a canter—a canter's the pace,
　　The groom rides behind on his mare ;
With his livery trimmed with a handsome gold lace,
　　And his neat little cropped head of hair.

A gallop—a gallop—a gallop—a gallop,
    Here comes the old farmer behind ;
Now he goes down the hill, and see here he comes up,
    Till his nag has quite broken his wind.

My Castle

I had a castle built,
    At the bottom of the sea ;
It was a very pretty place,
    I think you will agree.

The windows were of coral,
    The doors of pearls were made ;
The staircase was of amber,
    The floors with shells were laid.

I took my little wife there,
    But soon I heard her say,
She'd rather live above the ground,
    And so she ran away.

The Naughty Girl

Sister's gone to gather posies,
Made of jessamines and roses ;
Brother to the fair is gone,
And I'm left here quite alone.
Heigh ho ! nonino !
    Nonny, nonny, nonino !
    When I grow a better girl,
    Mammy then will let me go.

Little girl, and why don't you
Go and gather posies too ?
Oh ! because I tore my frock,
And dirtied all my nice new book—
 Heigh ho ! nonino !
 Nonny, nonny, nonino !
 When I grow a better girl,
 Mammy then will let me go.

Two People of Fife

In a cottage near Fife,
Lived a man and his wife,
Who, believe me, were comical folk ;
For to people's surprise,
They both saw with their eyes,
And their tongues moved, whenever they spoke.

What's amazing to tell,
I have heard that their smell
Chiefly lay in a thing called their nose.
And, though strange are such tales,
On their fingers they'd nails,
As well as on each of their toes.

When quite fast asleep,
I've been told that to keep
Their eyes open they scarce could contrive ;
They walked on their feet,
And 'twas thought, what they eat
Helped, with drinking, to keep them alive.

The Teacher

Come hither, little piggy wiggy,
    come and learn your letters,
And you shall have a knife and fork
    to eat with, like your betters.
No, no ! the little pig replied,
    my trough will do as well,
I'd rather eat my victuals there,
    than go and learn to spell.
With a tingle, tangle, titmouse !
    Robin knows great A,
And B, and C, and D, and E,
    F, G, H, I, J, K.

Come hither, little puppy dog,
    and be a clever scholar,
If you will learn to read your book,
    I'll give you a new collar.
No, no ! replied the puppy dog,
    I've other fish to fry ;
For I must learn to guard your house,
    and bark when thieves come nigh.

With a tingle, tangle, titmouse !
    Robin knows great A,
And B, and C, and D, and E,
    F, G, H, I, J, K.

Come hither, little pussy cat,
    if you'll your grammar study,
I'll give you silver clogs to wear,
    whene'er the gutter's muddy.
No ! whilst I grammar learn, says puss,
    your house will in a trice,
Be over-run, from top to bottom,
    with the rats and mice.
With a tingle, tangle, titmouse !
    Robin knows great A,
And B, and C, and D, and E,
    F, G, H, I, J, K.

Come hither then, good little boy,
  and learn your alphabet,
And you a pair of boots and spurs,
  like your papa's shall get.
Oh yes ! I'll learn my alphabet,
  and when I well can read,
Perhaps papa will give me too,
  a pretty long-tailed steed.
With a tingle, tangle, titmouse !
  Robin knows great A,
And B, and C, and D, and E,
  F, G, H, I, J, K.

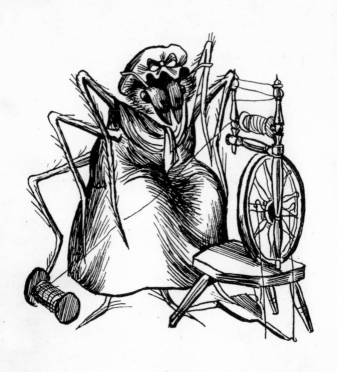

The Spider and the Fly

" Spider, spider ! what d'ye spin ? "
　　" Mainsails for a man of war ! "
" Spider, spider, it's too thin ;
　　Tell me truly what it's for ? "

" Why, good fly," the spider said,
    " It's for curtains for the king,
    When he sleeps in his state bed ! "
" Spider, it's too slight a thing ! "

" Slight ! Oh no ! your eyes deceive ! "
    Said the spider to the fly ;
      " Strong and firm, and tight I weave !
Come, examine !—touch and try."

" Cunning spider ! 'twill not do,
    Of your arts I am aware ;
Grandma cautioned me of you,
    And told me why you spread
            your snare."

A Long Story

John and his mare a journey went,
    Humble, dumble, derry, derry, dee !
They travelled slow, by joint consent,
    Tweedle, tweedle, tweedle, twinery !

They travelled near a hundred miles,
    Humble, dumble, derry, derry, dee !
The mare leaped over all the stiles,
    Tweedle, tweedle, tweedle, twinery !

It rained and blew as night came on,
    Humble, dumble, derry, derry, dee !
" I wish we were at home," said John,
    Tweedle, tweedle, tweedle, twinery !

" We've lost our way, so dark it grows,"
    Humble, dumble, derry, derry, dee !
" I cannot even see my nose,"
    Tweedle, tweedle, tweedle, twinery !

Says the mare, " What shall I do ? "
    Humble, dumble, derry, derry, dee !
" Master, I have lost my shoe ! "
    Tweedle, tweedle, tweedle, twinery !

" Good lack ! " says John, " where can we stop ?"
    Humble, dumble, derry, derry, dee !
" I cannot see a blacksmith's shop ! "
    Tweedle, tweedle, tweedle, twinery !

At length they came to a great hall,
    Humble, dumble, derry, derry, dee !
Where John did loudly knock and call,
    Tweedle, tweedle, tweedle, twinery !

The king came out, all dressed so gay,
    Humble, dumble, derry, derry, dee !
And begged to know, what he'd to say,
    Tweedle, tweedle, tweedle, twinery !

Says John, " I'm wet, Sir, to the skin,"
    Humble, dumble, derry, derry, dee !
" Oh," says the king, " good Sir, come in,"
    Tweedle, tweedle, tweedle, twinery !

The king brought a dry shirt to John,
    Humble, dumble, derry, derry, dee !
And helped him to put it on,
    Tweedle, tweedle, tweedle, twinery !

He introduced him to the queen,
    Humble, dumble, derry, derry, dee !
As fine a dame as e'er was seen,
    Tweedle, tweedle, tweedle, twinery !

The queen stepped down, from off her throne,
    Humble, dumble, derry, derry, dee !
Shook hands and said, " You're welcome John
    Tweedle, tweedle, tweedle, twinery !

They gave him supper, and a bed,
    Humble, dumble, derry, derry, dee !
And ordered that his horse be fed,
    Tweedle, tweedle, tweedle, twinery !

So well did John behave him there,
    Humble, dumble, derry, derry, dee !
The king and queen made him lord-mayor,
    Tweedle, tweedle, tweedle, twinery !

And now he's got a coach and four,
    Humble, dumble, derry, derry, dee !
I'll end my song, and sing no more,
    Tweedle, tweedle, tweedle, twinery !

What of That?

Polly Piper plucked a pigeon,
    Charley Chester choked a cat ;
Willy Wimble winged a widgeon,
    Well, good Sir, and what of that ?

Polly Piper's papa praised her,
  Charley's cousin cracked his crown ;
Willy's wife said Will amazed her,
  Now, good Sir, you're wiser grown.

The Letters

A, B, C,
Were grieved to see
That D, E, F,
Were very deaf ;
So bid G, H,
A doctor fetch,
Who told I, J,
Some salve to lay.
On this, K, L,
Said they knew well
That M, N, O,
More skill did show ;
So asked P, Q,
To fetch them too ;
Which R, and S,
Did much distress,
As they and T,
Must pay the fee—
This U declar'd
Was very hard,
So sent for V,
To know if he
And W, X, and Y
Would try
To bribe old Z,
To pay instead.

The Little Jackdaw

See saw ! a little Jackdaw,
On the church-steeple, sat crying out " Caw ! "
    When the bells began to ring,
    The little Jackdaw he took wing,
And said he thought it vastly wrong,
The noisy bells should spoil his song !

See saw ! the little Jackdaw,
Filled his bill with hay and straw.
    Up he flew and crammed it tightly,
    In the bells that rang so sprightly,
And when he their sound had stopped,
Again up to the steeple hopped.

A New Moon

High diddledy doon,
  We have got a new moon ;
With a smart pair of horns, I declare !
  Like silver so fine,
  See how she does shine,
I should like her to stick in my hair.

High diddledy doon,
  Now we've got a new moon,
Where's the old one that we had before ?
  Oh ! without any doubt,
  They've in stars cut her out ;
There was plenty to make us a score.

Soldier

Soldier ! O Soldier ! in your fine red coat,
  Pray what are you going to do ?
      The French I will fight,
      And before it is night,
You shall see them all beat black and blue !
                            Black and blue !
You shall see them beat black and blue !

The Eggs

" How d'ye sell your eggs, my dear ? "
    " A dozen for a shilling !
But you shall have thirteen, I swear,
    If you to buy are willing."

" Come count them out, good damsel, then,
    Whilst I the best am picking ;
I'll put them underneath a hen,
    And she shall hatch a chicken."

At six weeks end, lo ! and behold !
    When they came to examine ;
They found the eggs were stuffed with gold
    So full, no more could cram in !

The Unwise Owl

In an oak there lived an owl,
    Frisky, whisky, wheedle !
She thought herself a clever fowl;
    Fiddle, faddle, feedle.

Her face alone her wisdom shew,
    Frisky, whisky, wheedle !
For all she said was " whit te whoo ! "
    Fiddle, faddle, feedle.

Her silly note a gunner heard,
    Frisky, whisky, wheedle !
Says he, " I'll shoot you, stupid bird ! "
    Fiddle, faddle, feedle.

Now if he had not heard her hoot,
    Frisky, whisky, wheedle !
He had not found her out to shoot,
    Fiddle, faddle, feedle.

Cobbler, Cobbler

" Cobbler, cobbler, mend my shoe."
" Yes, good master, that I'll do ;
Here's my awl and my wax thread,
And now your shoe is quite mended."

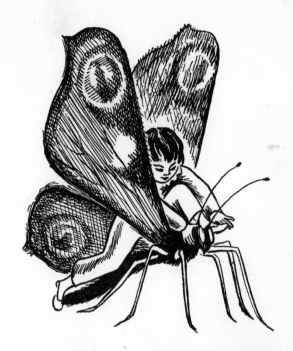

Billy and the Butterfly

Billy he mounted a butterfly's back,
    Hepity, lepity, lee !
And he flew to the top of a new-made hay-stack,
    With a high dumble, dumble, derree !

"Odds bobs !" said a crow, whom they found sitting
                                there,
    Hepity, lepity, lee !
"Don't disturb me I beg, for no place can I spare !"
    With a high dumble, dumble, derree !

So away they both flew, till at length they did perch
      Hepity, lepity, lee !
On the top of the steeple of Chichester church,
      With a high dumble, dumble, derree !

A dozen old jackdaws came pounce round their ears,
      Hepity, lepity, lee !
And bid them depart, for the steeple was theirs,
      With a high dumble, dumble, derree !

Billy thought it was hard to be thus turned away,
      Hepity, lepity, lee !
So vowed that in spite of them all, he would stay,
      With a high dumble, dumble, derree !

The biggest old jackdaw flew smack at his nose,
      Hepity, lepity, lee !
Whilst the others all pecked at his fingers and toes,
      With a high dumble, dumble, derree !

Poor Billy called out, in most grievous dismay,
      Hepity, lepity, lee !
And was glad to make off, without saying good day,
      With a high dumble, dumble, derree !

They rested no more till they came to a star,
    Hepity, lepity, lee !
Where they begged they might stop, as they'd travelled
                              so far,

    With a high dumble, dumble, derree !

The star could not hold them, so higher they rose,
    Hepity, lepity, lee !
Till they came to the sun, who burnt off Billy's clothes,
    With a high dumble, dumble, derree !

" Alas ! " says poor Billy, " I'll venture no more ! "
    Hepity, lepity, lee !
" What business had I from my station to soar,"
    With a high dumble, dumble, derree !

Robin Hood

" Pray who did kill that noble stag ? "
" 'Twas I !—'twas I !—'twas I !
And I am called bold Robin Hood ! "
" Bold Robin, you must die."

Then Robin laughed and whistled loud,
    And straight his archers came ;
They ducked the verderer in a pool,
    And laughed to see his shame.

Cock a Doodle Doodle Doo

Cock a doodle doodle doo,
    Cock a doodle dandy !
I have got a pretty maid,
    And she is very handy.
She washes all her knives and forks,
    And platters in the sea, Sir ;
She scrubs the floor with cabbage stalks,
    As clean as clean can be, Sir.

Cock a doodle doodle doo,
    Cock a doodle didy !
I have got a pretty maid,
    And she is very tidy.
She sweeps the cobwebs off the sky,
    And rubs with all her might, Sir,
The sun, and moon, and stars so high,
    Or how would they look bright, Sir ?

The Invalid

" Why is pussy in bed ? "
    " She's sick," says the fly,
    " And I fear she will die !
That's why she's in bed ! "

" Pray what's her disorder ? "
    " She's got a locked jaw,"
    Says the little jackdaw,
" And that's her disorder."

48

" Who makes her gruel ? "
" I," says the horse,
" For I am her nurse,
And I make her gruel."

" Pray who is her doctor ? "
  " Quack ! quack ! " says the duck,
  " I that task undertook,
And I am her doctor."

" Who pays the fee ? "
  " I," says the bitch,
  " Because I am rich,
So I pay the fee."

" Who thinks she'll recover ? "
  " I," says the deer,
  " For I did last year,
So I think she'll recover."

The Man in the Moon

Pray tell me how the man in the moon
    Contrives his time to kill, Sir?
For, since he lives there quite alone,
    It must require some skill, Sir.

Oh! though his pastimes are but scarce,
    He's at no loss for fun, Sir;
He plays at marbles with the stars,
    And trap-ball with the sun, Sir.

Barbara Brittle

Barbara Brittle,
Suits me to a tittle,
For she loves fat bacon and ale ;
But if none she can get,
Why she never does fret,
For she knows it will nothing avail.

Barbara Brittle,
Suits me to a tittle,
When sleeping she never does snore ;
If she did with the clothes
I would cork up her nose,
And I never would sleep with her more.

The Quarrel

Tweedledum and Tweedledee
    Agreed to fight a battle ;
For Tweedledum, said Tweedledee,
    Had spoiled his nice new rattle.

Just then flew down a monstrous crow,
    As black as a tar barrel ;
Which frightened both the heroes so,
    They quite forgot their quarrel.

The Inheritance

My mother she died, and she left me a reel,
A little silver thimble, and a pretty spinning-wheel ;
With a high down, derry O, derry O, derry O !
High down, derry O ! dance o'er the broom.

I spun all day, and I sold my yarn,
And I put in my purse all the money I did earn ;
With a high down, derry O, derry O, derry O !
High down, derry O ! dance o'er the broom.

And when at last I'd saved enough,
I bought me a gown of a pretty silver stuff ;
With a high down, derry O, derry O, derry O !
High down, derry O ! dance o'er the broom.

A cap of gold, and a sash so gay !
" O what a pretty lady ! " I heard the people say ;
With a high down, derry O, derry O, derry O !
High down, derry O ! dance o'er the broom.

Had I been idle, then no doubt,
In rags, like a beggar, I'd wandered about ;
With a high down, derry O, derry O, derry O !
High down, derry O ! dance o'er the broom.

The Sportsman

I had a little gun, 'twas no bigger than a pen,
I fired it through a hedge and I shot a little hen ;
I meant to eat it up, but indeed it was so pretty,
I thought to pluck and roast it, would be a shocking pity
Its feathers were of silver, its head was made of gold,
I knew it would fetch money, so I sent it to be sold.

The Bells of London

The bells in London all fell wrangling,
One said t'other made such jangling.

Whitechapel's did the strife begin,
By bidding Shoreditch cease her din !

St. Clement's bells abused St. Martin's,
Said they were not worth five farthings.

St. Aldgate's said, St. Clement's chimes,
She'd swear, were worse a thousand times.

" Oh, hold your clappers ! " said St. John's,
" Why need you make comparisons ?
You are all like warming pans,
As bad, or worse than poor St. Ann's ! "

On this St. Ann's protested loud,
St. John's herself need not be proud—

" Why what the deuce, good folks, can ail ye ? "
Said the bells of the Old Bailey ;
" How the pot becalls the kettle :
You're all made of shocking metal ! "

" Zooks ! " says the great bell of Bow,
" Do you presume your taste to show !
When nothing worse than yours can be,
Except, indeed, those of Stepney ! "

Says Stepney's bells, " Who would suppose
That Bow could thus turn up her nose ?
A proverb she, with all her jeers,
That breaks the drums of people's ears ! "

St. Giles's bells, politely here,
Requested they might interfere ;
And thought the rest rung vastly well,
Though none could yet her own excel.

The Blue Fly

Buz ! buz ! quoth the great blue fly,
Who is so happy, so happy as I ?
    I whisk through the air,
     Without thought, without care,
And no king is so happy as I, as I !
And no king is so happy as I.

Tabitha Roe

Heigh ho ! Tabitha Roe,
Walking to market was caught in the snow ;
    Poor Miss Tabby ! fie upon it !
    Quite forgot to wear her bonnet ;
So she caught a cold in her head,
And for a whole week lay sick in her bed.

Heigh ho ! Tabitha Roe,
Let fall the kettle and scalded her toe ;
    When the doctor came to dress it,
    He did sadly pinch and press it ;
But had Tabitha taken care,
No doctor had been wanted there.

Granny Huet and Daddy Dacon

Old Granny Huet,
She lived upon suet,
Till she was as fat as a pig.
She cut off her hair,
To make the folks stare,
And then wore a little bob wig.

Old Daddy Dacon,
He lived upon bacon,
Till bristles grew out of his nose.
There came by a thrush,
Who believed it a bush,
And built a snug nest for repose.

Old Granny Huet,
Who lived upon suet,
She put her bob wig on one side ;
And then looked so smart,
That she won Daddy's heart,
Who protested he'd make her his bride.

Daddy Dacon's old thrush,
Who had built in the bush
On his nose, laid some eggs in her nest ;
Which Old Granny Huet
Did fry with her suet,
Declaring they'd make it digest.

The Concert

Little Tommy Titmouse sat on Jenny's knee,
He sang tweedledum, and she sang tweedledee !
Tweedle, tweedle, tweedle, both sang through their nose,
The dog he joined the concert with three great loud
bow wows ;
The cat jumped up with wonder, and frightened ran
away
Believing it was thunder, she dared no longer stay !

Peter Prim

" Peter Prim !   Peter Prim !
Why do you in stockings swim ? "

Peter Prim gave this reply,
" To make such fools as you ask why ! "

Mother Bulletout

What an odd dame Mother Bulletout's grown !
She dresses her ducks and her drakes in cocked hats
Her hens wear hoop petticoats made of whalebon
And she puts little breeches on all her Tom cats.

Mother Shuttle

Old Mother Shuttle
Lived in a coal-scuttle,
Along with her dog and her cat ;
What they ate I can't tell,
But 'tis known very well,
That not one of the party was fat.

Old Mother Shuttle
Scoured out her coal-scuttle,
And washed both her dog and her cat ;
The cat scratched her nose,
So they came to hard blows,
And who was the gainer by that ?

A Journey on a Broom

There was an old woman, who rode on a broom,
    With a high gee ho ! gee humble,
And she took her Tom Cat behind for a groom,
    With a bimble, bamble, bumble.

They travelled along till they came to the sky,
    With a high gee ho! gee humble,
But the journey so long made them very hungry,
    With a bimble, bamble, bumble.

Says Tom, " I can find nothing here to eat,
    With a high gee ho ! gee humble,
So let us go back again, I entreat !
    With a bimble, bamble, bumble."

The old woman would not go back so soon,
    With a high gee ho ! gee humble,
For she wanted to visit the man in the moon
    With a bimble, bamble, bumble.

" Then," says Tom, " I'll go back by myself to our
                          house,
    With a high gee ho ! gee humble,
For there I can catch a good rat or a mouse,
    With a bimble, bamble, bumble."

" But," says the old woman, " how will you go ?
    With a high gee ho ! gee humble,
You shan't have my nag, I protest and vow !
    With a bimble, bamble, bumble."

" No, no," says old Tom, " I've a plan of my own,
    With a high gee ho ! gee humble."
So he slid down the rainbow, and left her alone,
    With a bimble, bamble, bumble.

70

Jenny Flinders

Little Jenny Flinders
Sat in the cinders,
Warming her poor little toes ;
Her mammy came and caught her,
And whipped her little daughter,
For spoiling her nice new clothes.

The Farmer

A farmer went trotting upon his grey mare,
 Bumpety, bumpety, bump !
With his daughter behind him so rosy and fair,
 Lumpety, lumpety, lump !

A magpie cried " Caw " and they all tumbled down,
 Bumpety, bumpety, bump !
The mare broke her knees, and the farmer his crown,
 Lumpety, lumpety, lump !

The mischievous magpie flew laughing away,
 Bumpety, bumpety, bump !
And vowed he would serve them the same the next day,
 Lumpety, lumpety, lump !

74

Green Cheese

here was an old woman who made green cheese,
    By beating up spinach and curds with a spoon ;
nd when she had done it, with very great ease,
    Tossed it up to the sky, and declared 'twas the moon.

'Squire Frog's Visit

'Squire Frog he went to Mouse's hall,
   "Heigh ho !" says Brittle !
'Squire Frog he went to Mouse's hall,
Dressed out quite smart for a supper and ball ;
    With a namby, pamby,
    Mannikin, pannikin,
    "Heigh !" says Barnaby Brittle !

Mr. Rat he bowed, and welcomed him in,
   "Heigh ho !" says Brittle !
Mr. Rat he bowed, and welcomed him in,
And all the Miss Mouses went curtseying ;
    With a namby, pamby,
    Mannikin, pannikin,
    "Heigh !" says Barnaby Brittle !

Then Rat did for the fiddlers call,
   "Heigh ho !" says Brittle !
Then Rat did for the fiddlers call,
And requested that Froggy would open the ball ;
    With a namby, pamby,
    Mannikin, pannikin,
    "Heigh !" says Barnaby Brittle !

Mrs. Mouse he took out in a minuet,
    " Heigh ho ! " says Brittle !
Mrs. Mouse he took out in a minuet,
And danced reels with the Misses, till quite
                          in a sweat ;
    With a namby, pamby,
    Mannikin, pannikin,
    " Heigh ! " says Barnaby Brittle !

They danced until the clock struck one,
    " Heigh ho ! " says Brittle !
They danced until the clock struck one,
When Rat said supper was begun ;
    With a namby, pamby,
    Mannikin, pannikin,
    " Heigh ! " says Barnaby Brittle !

" Good wife, pray hand that dish below,"
    " Heigh ho ! " says Brittle !
" Good wife, pray hand that dish below,
For Froggy and I love harico ; "
    With a namby, pamby,
    Mannikin, pannikin,
    " Heigh ! " says Barnaby Brittle !

" Pray give 'Squire Frog some currant tart,"
    " Heigh ho ! " says Brittle !
" Pray give 'Squire Frog some currant tart,"
And I will take the other part,
    With a namby, pamby,
    Mannikin, pannikin,
     " Heigh ! " says Barnaby Brittle !

" Go fetch the wine from off the hob,"
    " Heigh ho ! " says Brittle !
" Go fetch the wine from off the hob,
For Froggy and I must have a hob-nob ; "
    With a namby, pamby,
    Mannikin, pannikin,
     " Heigh ! " says Barnaby Brittle !

Then Frog he begged to give a toast,
    " Heigh ho ! " says Brittle !
Then Frog he begged to give a toast,
" MAY THE FRENCH NEVER FRICASSEE
             ME ON OUR COAST ! "
    With a namby, pamby,
    Mannikin, pannikin,
     " Heigh ! " says Barnaby Brittle !

Whilst thus they merry-making sat,
    " Heigh ho ! " says Brittle !
Whilst thus they merry-making sat,
Came bouncing in the great black cat,
    With a namby, pamby,
    Mannikin, pannikin,
     " Heigh ! " says Barnaby Brittle !

He seized the old rat in a trice,
    " Heigh ho ! " says Brittle !
He seized the old rat in a trice,
And vengeance was vowed on all the mice ;
    With a namby, pamby,
    Mannikin, pannikin,
    " Heigh ! " says Barnaby Brittle !

When Froggy saw their dismal plight,
    " Heigh ho ! " says Brittle !
When Froggy saw their dismal plight,
He thought 'twould be wiser to wish them good nigh
    With a namby, pamby,
    Mannikin, pannikin,
    " Heigh ! " says Barnaby Brittle !

809